Enid Blyton®

A FARAWAY TREE
ADVENTURE

The Land of
DREAMS

h HODDER

The World of the FARAWAY TREE

MOON-FACE lives at the very top. In his house is the start of the **SLIPPERY-SLIP**, a huge slide that curves all the way down inside the trunk of the tree.

SILKY lives below Moon-Face. She is the prettiest little fairy you ever did see.

SAUCEPAN MAN is a funny old thing. His saucepans make lots of noise when they jangle together, so he can't hear very well.

A FARAWAY TREE
ADVENTURE

The Land of
DREAMS

For Sophia and Cece
A. P.

HODDER CHILDREN'S BOOKS
Text first published in Great Britain as chapters 9-11 of *The Magic Faraway Tree* in 1943
First published as *A Faraway Tree Adventure: The Land of Dreams* in 2017
by Egmont UK Limited
This edition published in 2021 by Hodder & Stoughton Limited

1 3 5 7 9 10 8 6 4 2

The Magic Faraway Tree ®, Enid Blyton ® and Enid Blyton's signature are registered
trade marks of Hodder & Stoughton Limited
Text © Hodder & Stoughton Limited
Cover and interior illustrations by Alex Paterson © Hodder & Stoughton Limited

A CIP catalogue record for this book is available from the British Library.

ISBN 978 1 444 95991 8

Printed and bound in China

The paper and board used in this book are made from wood from responsible sources.

Hodder Children's Books
An imprint of
Hachette Children's Group
Part of Hodder & Stoughton
Carmelite House
50 Victoria Embankment
London EC4Y 0DZ

An Hachette UK Company
www.hachette.co.uk
www.hachettechildrens.co.uk

CHAPTER ONE
Enough Adventures

The children had **had enough of adventures** for some time. Their mother set them to work in the garden, and they did their best for her. Nobody suggested going to the Enchanted Wood at all.

'I hope old Moon-Face, Silky and the Saucepan Man got back to the tree safely,' said Joe one day.

Moon-Face was wondering the same thing about the children. He and Silky talked about it.

'**We haven't seen the children for ages**,' he said. 'Let's slip down the tree, Silky, and make sure they got back all right, shall we? After all, it would be dreadful if they hadn't got back, and their mother was worrying about them.'

So one afternoon, just after lunch, Silky, Moon-Face and the Saucepan Man walked up to the door of the cottage. Beth opened it and **shrieked with delight**.

'Moon-Face! So you got back safely after all! **Come in!** Come in, Silky dear. Saucepan, you'll have to take off a kettle or two if you want to get through the door.'

The children's parents were out for a while. The children and their friends sat and talked about their last adventure.

'What land is at the top of the tree now?' asked Rick curiously.

'Don't know,' said Moon-Face. 'Like to come and see?'

'No, thanks,' said Joe at once. 'We're not going up there any more.'

'Well, come back and have tea with us,' said Moon-Face. 'Silky's got some Pop Cakes – and **I've made some Google Buns.** I don't often make them – and I tell you they're a treat!'

'Google Buns!' said Beth in astonishment. '**Whatever are they?**'

'You come and see,' said Moon-Face, grinning. 'They're better than Pop Cakes – aren't they, Silky?'

'Much,' said Silky.

'Well – Frannie and I have finished our jobs,' said Beth. 'What about you boys?'

'We've got about half an hour's more work to do, that's all,' said Joe. 'If everyone helps, it will only take ten minutes. We could leave a note for Mother and Father. I would love to try those Google Buns!'

Everyone went into the garden to dig up the carrots and put them into piles. It didn't take more than ten minutes because **they all worked so hard**. They put away their tools, washed their hands, left a note for their parents, and **then set off for the Enchanted Wood**.

Then Saucepan Man sang one of his ridiculous songs on the way:

'Two tails for a kitten,

Two clouds for the sky,

Two pigeons for Christmas,

To make a plum pie!'

Everyone laughed. Joe, Beth and Frannie had heard the Saucepan Man's silly songs before, but Rick hadn't. 'Go on,' said Rick. 'This is **the silliest song I've ever heard**.'

The Saucepan Man clashed two kettles together as he sang:

'Two roses for Beth,

Two scoldings for Joe,

Two ribbons for Frannie,

With a ho-diddle-ho!'

'It's an easy song to make up as you go along,' said Beth, giggling. 'Every line but the last has to begin with the word "Two". Just **think of any nonsense you like**, and the song simply makes itself.'

Singing silly songs, they all reached the Faraway Tree. Saucepan yelled up it:

'Hey, Watzisname! Let down a rope, there's a good fellow! It's too hot to walk up today.'

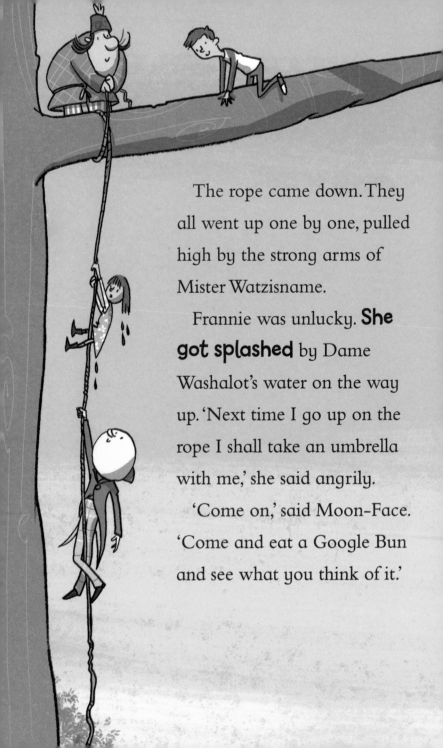

The rope came down. They all went up one by one, pulled high by the strong arms of Mister Watzisname.

Frannie was unlucky. **She got splashed** by Dame Washalot's water on the way up. 'Next time I go up on the rope I shall take an umbrella with me,' she said angrily.

'Come on,' said Moon-Face. 'Come and eat a Google Bun and see what you think of it.'

CHAPTER TWO
The Land of Dreams

Soon they were all sitting on the broad branches outside Moon-Face's house, eating **Pop Cakes and Google Buns**. The buns were very strange. They each had a very large raisin in the middle, and this was filled with sherbet. So when you got to the raisin and bit it the sherbet frothed out and filled your mouth with fine bubbles that tasted **delicious**.

The children got a real surprise when they bit their raisins, and Moon-Face almost fell off the branch with laughing.

'Come and see some new cushions I've got,' he said to the children when they had **eaten as many cakes and buns as they could manage**. Joe, Beth and Frannie went into Moon-Face's funny round house.

Moon-Face looked round for Rick. But he

wasn't there. '**Where's Rick?**' he said.

'He's gone up the ladder to peep and see what land is at the top,' said Silky. 'I told him not to. But he's quite a **naughty boy,** I think.'

'Gosh,' said Joe, running out of the house. 'Rick, come back, you silly!'

Everyone began to shout, 'Rick, RICK!'

But no answer came down the ladder. The big white cloud swirled above silently,

and nobody could imagine why Rick didn't come back. '**I'll go and see what he's doing**,' said Moon-Face.

So up he went. And he didn't come back either! Then the Old Saucepan Man went cautiously up, step by step. He disappeared through the hole – **and he didn't come back!**

'Whatever has happened to them?' said Joe in despair. 'Look here, girls – get a rope out of Moon-Face's house and tie yourselves and Silky to me. Then I'll go up the ladder – and if anyone tries to pull me into the land above, they won't be able to, because you three can pull me back. OK?'

'Right,' said
Beth, and she
knotted the rope
round her waist
and Frannie's,
and then round
Silky's too. Joe tied
the other end to
himself. Then up
the ladder he went.

And before the girls knew what had
happened, Joe was lifted into the land above
– and they were all dragged up, too, their
feet scrambling somehow up the ladder and
through the hole in the cloud!

There they all stood in a field of red
poppies, with a tall man nearby, holding a
sack over his shoulder!

'Is that the lot?' he asked. 'Good! Well, here's
something to **make you sleep!**'

He put his hand in his sack and scattered a handful of the finest sand over the surprised group. In a moment they were rubbing their eyes and yawning.

'**This is the Land of Dreams**,' said Moon-Face sleepily. '**And that's the Sandman**. Goodness, how sleepy I am!'

'Don't go to sleep! **Don't go to sleep!**'
cried Silky, taking Moon-Face's arm and
shaking him. 'If we do, we'll wake up and
find that this land has moved away from the
Faraway Tree. **Come back down the hole**,
Moon-Face, and don't be silly.'

'I'm so – sleepy,' said Moon-Face, and lay
down among the red poppies. In no time he
was snoring loudly, fast asleep.

'**Get him to the hole!**' cried Silky. But Joe, Rick and the Saucepan Man were all yawning and rubbing their eyes, **too sleepy to do a thing**. Then Beth and Frannie slid down quietly into the poppies and fell asleep, too. At last only Silky was left. Not much of the sleepy sand had gone into her eyes, so she was wider awake than the rest.

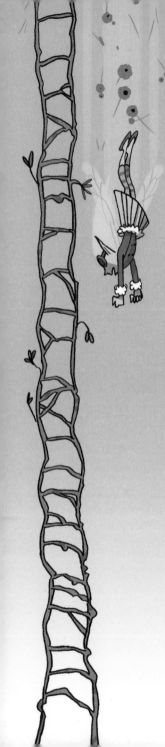

She stared at everyone in dismay. '**Oh dear**,' she said, 'I'll never get you down the hole by myself. **I'll have to get help**. I must go and fetch Watzisname and the Angry Pixie and Dame Washalot, too!'

She ran off to the hole, slipped down the ladder through the cloud and slid on to the broad branch below. 'Watzisname!' she called. 'Dame Washalot! Angry Pixie!'

CHAPTER THREE
Ice-cream, Marbles and a Swimming Pool

After a minute or two **Joe woke up**. He rubbed his eyes and sat up. Not far off he saw something that pleased him. It was an **ice-cream seller**. The man was ringing his bell loudly.

'Hey, Moon-Face! Wake up!' cried Joe. 'There's an ice-cream man. Have you got any money?'

Everyone woke up. Moon-Face felt in his money bag and then stared in great surprise. **It was full of marbles.**

'Now who put marbles there?' he wondered.

The ice-cream man drove up. '**Marbles will do to pay for my ice-cream**,' he said.
So Moon-Face paid him six marbles.

The man gave them each a bag and drove off, ringing his bell. **Moon-Face opened his bag**, expecting to find a delicious ice-cream there – **but inside there was a big whistle!** It was really odd.

Everyone else had a whistle too. 'How extraordinary!' said Rick. **'This is the kind of thing that happens in dreams!'**

'Well – after all – **this is Dreamland!'** said Beth. 'I wonder if these whistles blow!'

She blew hers. It was very loud indeed.
The others blew theirs, too. And at once **six
policemen appeared** nearby, running for
all they were worth. They rushed up to the
children.

'What's the matter?' they cried. 'You are blowing police whistles! What has happened? **Do you want help?**'

'No,' said Rick with a giggle.

'Then you must come to the swimming pool,' said the policeman, and to everyone's surprise they were all led away.

'**Why the swimming pool?**' said Frannie. 'Listen, policeman – we haven't got swim-suits.'

'Oh, you naughty story-teller!' said the policeman nearest to her.

And to Beth's surprise she found that she had on a blue and white swim-suit – and all the others had swim-suits too.

They came to the swimming pool – but **there was no water** in it at all. **'Get in and swim,'** said the policeman.

'There's no water,' said Rick. 'Don't be silly.'

And then, very suddenly, all the policemen began to cry – and in no time **the swimming pool was full of their tears!**

'This sort of thing makes me feel funny,' said Joe. '**I don't want to swim in tears.** Quick, everyone – push the policemen into the pool!'

And in half a second all the policemen were kicking feebly in the pool of tears. As the children watched they **changed into blue fishes and swam away**, flicking their tails.

'I feel as if I'm in a dream,' said Rick.

'So do I,' said Joe. 'I wish I could get out of it. Oh, look – **there's a plane** coming down. Perhaps we could get into it and fly away!'

The plane, which was small and green, landed near by. There was nobody in it at all. The children ran to it and got in. **Joe pushed down the handle marked UP.**

'Off we go!' he said. And off they went!

CHAPTER FOUR
A Few More Adventures

Everyone was very pleased to be in the plane, because they **thought they could fly away from the Land of Dreams**. After a second or two Beth leaned over the side of the plane to see how high they were from the ground. She gave a loud cry.

'What's the matter?' asked Joe.

'**Joe! This isn't a plane after all!**' said Beth in astonishment. '**It's a bus**. It hasn't got wings any more. Only wheels. And we're sitting on seats at the top of the bus. Well! I did think it was a plane!'

'Gosh! Aren't we flying then?' said Joe.

'No – just running down a road,' said Frannie. Everyone was silent. They were **so disappointed**.

Then a curious noise was heard. **Splishy-splash! Splash! Splash!**

The children looked over the side of the bus – and they all gave a shout of amazement.

'Joe! Look! The bus is running on water! But **it isn't a bus any more**. Oh, look – it's got a sail!'

Everyone looked upwards – and there, **billowing in the wind, was a great white sail**. And Joe was now steering with a tiller instead of with a handle or a wheel. It was **very confusing**.

'This is **definitely the Land of Dreams**, no doubt about that,' groaned Joe, wondering whatever the ship would turn into next. 'The awful part is – we're awake – and yet we have to have these dream-like things happening!'

An enormous wave splashed over everyone. Frannie gave a scream. The ship rocked backwards and forwards, to and fro, and everyone clung tightly to one another.

39

'Let's land somewhere, for goodness' sake!' cried Rick. **Heaven knows what this ship will turn into next** – a rocking-horse, I should think, by the way it's rocking itself backwards and forwards.'

And, guess what? No sooner had Rick said that than **it did turn into a rocking-horse**.

Joe found himself holding on to its mane, and all the others clung together behind him. **The water disappeared.** The rocking-horse seemed to be rocking down a long road.

'**Let's get off**,' shouted Joe. 'I don't like the way this thing keeps changing. Slip off, Moon-Face, and help the others down.'

It wasn't long before they were all standing in the road, feeling rather confused. The rocking-horse went on rocking by itself down the road. As the children watched it, **it changed into a large brown bear** that scampered on its big paws.

'Ha!' said Joe. 'We got off just in time! Well – what are we going to do now?'

A man came down the road carrying a green-covered tray on his head. He rang a bell. 'Muffins! Fine muffins!' he shouted. '**Muffins for sale!**'

'Oooh! I really feel as if I could eat a muffin,' said Beth. '**Hey, muffin-man!** We'll have six muffins please.'

The muffin-man stopped. He took down his tray from his head and uncovered it. **Underneath were not muffins, but small kittens!** The muffin-man seemed to think they were muffins.

He handed one to each of the surprised children, and one to Moon-Face and Saucepan.

Then he covered up his tray again and went down the road ringing his bell.

'Well, **does he think we can eat kittens?**' said Beth. 'Oh, but aren't they dear little things? What are we going to do with them?'

'They seem to be **growing**,' said Joe in
surprise. And so they were. In a minute or two
the kittens were too heavy to carry – they
were big cats! They still went on growing, and
soon they were as big as tigers. They
played around the children, who were really
rather afraid of them.

'Now listen,' said Joe to the enormous kittens. 'You belong to the muffin-man. You go after him and get on to his tray where you belong. Listen – you can still hear his bell! **Go along now!**'

To everyone's surprise and delight the great animals ran off down the road after the muffin-man.

'He will get a surprise,' said Rick with a giggle. 'Hey – don't let's buy anything from anyone else. **It's a bit too risky**.'

CHAPTER FIVE
How to Get Home

'What we really should do is try and find the hole that leads from this land to the Faraway Tree,' said Joe seriously. '**Surely you don't want to stay in this peculiar land for ever!** Gosh, we never know what is happening from one minute to the next!'

'I feel very sleepy again,' said Moon-Face, yawning. 'I do wish I could go to bed.'

Just as he said that, there came a **clippitty-cloppitty** noise behind them. They all turned – and to their amazement saw a **big white bed** following them, trotting along on four fat legs.

'Gosh!' said Rick, stopping in surprise. 'Look at that bed! Where did it come from?'

The bed stopped just by them. Moon-Face yawned.

'I'd like to cuddle down in you and go to sleep,' he said to the bed. The bed **creaked** as if it was pleased.

Moon-Face climbed on to it. It was soft and cosy.

Moon-Face put his head on the pillow and shut his eyes. He began to snore very gently.

This made everyone else feel tired and sleepy too.

One by one they climbed into the big bed and lay down. The bed **creaked** in a very happy way. Then it went on its way again, **clippitty-clopping** on its four fat legs, taking the six sleepers with it.

Now what had happened to Silky?

Well, she had found Dame Washalot, Mister Watzisname and the Angry Pixie, and had told them how the others had fallen asleep in the Land of Dreams.

'Oh, good heavens! They'll never get away from there!' said Watzisname anxiously. '**We must rescue them**. Come along.'

Dame Washlot put a wash-tub of water on her head. The Angry Pixie picked up a kettle of water. Watzisname didn't take anything. **They all went up to the ladder** at the top of the tree.

'The Land of Dreams is still here,' said Silky when her head peeped over the top. 'I can't see that horrid Sandman anywhere. Now's a good chance to slip up and rescue the others. Come on!'

Up they all went. They stared round the field of poppies, but they couldn't see any of the others.

'**We must hunt for them**,' said Silky. 'Oh, look at that great brown bear rushing along! I wonder if he knows anything about the others.' She called out to him, but he didn't stop. He **made a noise like a chicken** and rushed on. The four of them wandered on and on – and suddenly they saw something very puzzling coming towards them – something wide and white.

'Whatever can it be?' said Silky in wonder. **'Goodness me – it's a BED!'**

And so it was – the very bed in which the four children and Moon-Face and Saucepan were asleep!

'Oh, look!' squealed Silky. **'They're all here!** Wake up, sillies! Wake up!'

But **they wouldn't wake up.** They just sighed a little and turned over. Nothing that Silky and the others could do would wake them up. And, in the middle of all this, there came footsteps behind them.

Silky turned round and gasped. 'Oh, it's the Sandman! Don't let him throw his sand into your eyes or you will go to sleep, too! **Quick, do something!**'

CHAPTER SIX
The Sandman

The Sandman was already dipping his hand into his big sack to throw sand into their eyes. But, **quick as lightning**, Dame Washalot picked up her wash-tub and threw all the water over the sack! It wetted the sand so that **the Sandman couldn't throw it properly**. Then the Angry Pixie emptied his kettle over the Sandman himself, and he began to choke and splutter.

Watzisname stared. He suddenly took out his small pocket scissors and cut a hole at the bottom of the sack. The sand was dry there. Watzisname took a handful of it and threw it at the spluttering Sandman's eyes.

'**Now you go to sleep** for a bit!' shouted Watzisname. And, of course, that's just what the big Sandman did! He sank down under a bush and shut his eyes. His sleepy sand acted on him as much as on anyone else!

'Now we've got a chance!' said Silky, pleased. '**Help me to wake everyone up!**'

But, you know, they just would not wake up! **It was impossible!**

'Well, we can't possibly get the bed down the hole,' said Silky in despair. Then a bright idea came to her. She felt in Joe's pockets. She turned out the little pink jar of whizz-away ointment. 'There might be just a little left!' she said.

And there was – the very tiniest dab! 'I hope it's enough!' said Silky. 'Get on the bed, Dame Washalot and you others. I'm going to try a little magic. Ready?'

She rubbed the dab of ointment on to the head of the bed. '**Whizz-Away Home, bed!**' she said.

And, wow, that big white bed **whizzed** away. It whizzed away so fast that Silky nearly fell off. It rushed through the air, giving all the birds a dreadful scare.

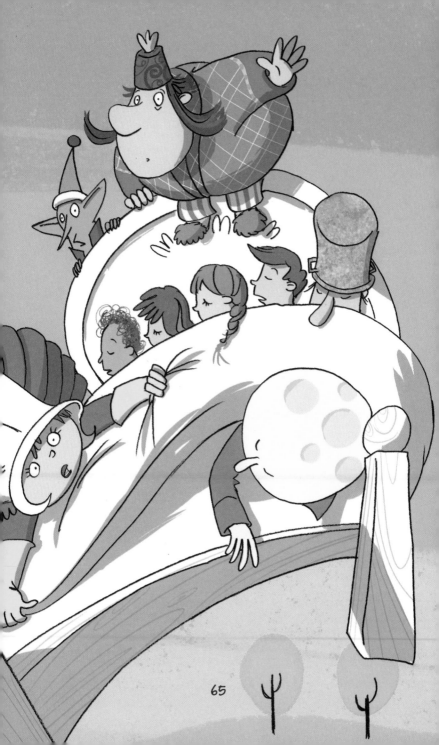

After a long time it came to the end of the
Land of Dreams. A big white cloud stretched
out at the edge. The bed flew through it, down
and down. Then it flew in another direction.

'It's going back to the Faraway Tree, I'm
sure,' said Silky. And so it was! It arrived there
and tried to get through the branches. It stuck
on one and slid sideways. Everyone began to
slide off.

'**Wake up, wake up!**' squealed Silky,
shaking the children and Moon-Face and
Saucepan. They woke up in a hurry, as **they
were no longer in Dreamland**. They
felt themselves falling and caught hold of
branches and twigs.

66

'Where are we?' cried Rick. 'What has happened?'

'Oh, goodness, **too many things to tell you all at once**,' said Silky. 'Is everyone safe? Then for goodness' sake come into my house and sit down for a bit. I really feel quite out of breath!'

Everyone crowded into Silky's room inside the tree. **'How did we get back to the tree?'** asked Rick in amazement.

Silky told him. 'We found you all asleep on that big bed, and we rubbed some of the **whizz-away ointment** on it, the very last bit left. And it whizzed away here. Oh, and we wetted the Sandman's sand so that he couldn't throw sand into our eyes and make us go to sleep.'

'Watzisname was clever, too. He cut the bottom of the sack with his scissors, found a handful of dry sand there and threw it at the Sandman himself!' said the Angry Pixie. 'And he went right off to sleep and couldn't use his powers on us any more!'

'**It was all Rick's fault**,' said Joe. 'We said we wouldn't go to any more lands – and he went up there and got caught by the Sandman. So of course we had to go after him.'

'**Sorry**,' said Rick. 'Anyway, everything's all right now. **I won't do it again.**'

'We'd better go home,' said Beth. 'It must be getting late. Goodness knows when we'll come again, Silky. **Goodbye everyone. Come and see us** if we don't come to see you.'

They all slid down the slippery-slip at top
speed. **Then they walked home**, talking
about their latest adventure.